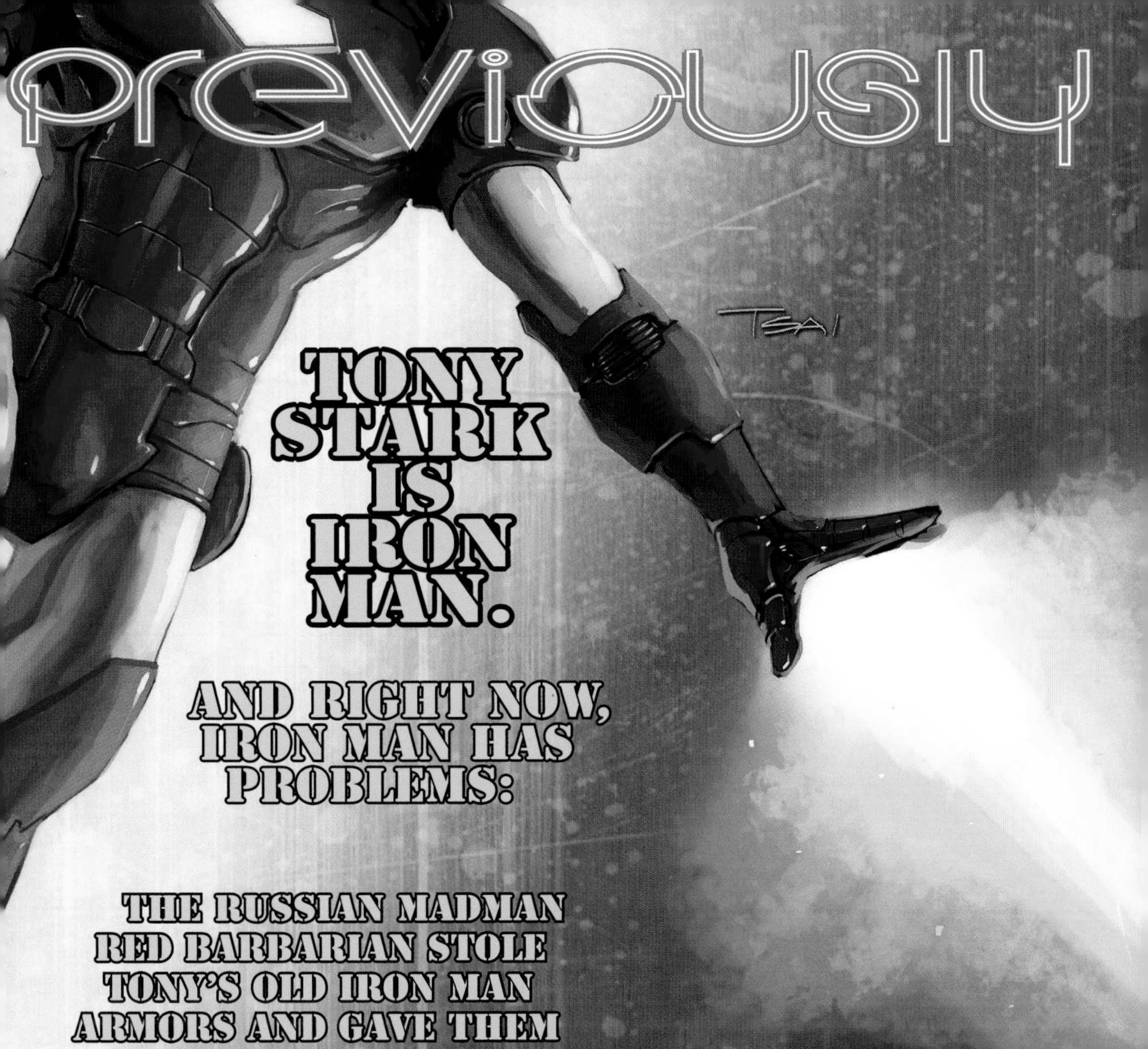
TSAI

previously

TONY STARK IS IRON MAN.

AND RIGHT NOW, IRON MAN HAS PROBLEMS:

THE RUSSIAN MADMAN RED BARBARIAN STOLE TONY'S OLD IRON MAN ARMORS AND GAVE THEM TO SUPER VILLAINS...

BARBARIAN ALSO STOLE TONY'S NEW NON-LETHAL PEACEKEEPER ARMOR, WHICH THE GOVERNMENT PAID FIVE BILLION DOLLARS FOR. THE GOVERNMENT BLAMES TONY...

...FORCING HIM TO GO ON THE RUN WITH HIS BEST FRIEND, RHODEY. THEY STOLE A PLANE, MISSILES WERE LAUNCHED, THINGS WENT BOOM...

THEN RHODEY (APPARENTLY) BETRAYED HIM...

WHICH IS WHY TONY'S CHAINED UP IN THE BARBARIAN'S LAIR...

IRON MAN AND THE ARMOR WARS™

JOE CARAMAGNA--WRITER
CRAIG ROUSSEAU--ART
VAL STAPLES--COLORS
DAVE SHARPE--LETTERS
TAKESHI MIYAZAWA--COVER
DAMIEN LUCCHESE--PRODUCTION
MICHAEL HORWITZ--ASST. EDITOR
NATHAN COSBY--EDITOR
JOE QUESADA--EDITOR IN CHIEF
DAN BUCKLEY--PUBLISHER
ALAN FINE--EXECUTIVE PRODUCER

MARVEL Spotlight

Part 4:

THE GOLDEN AVENGER STRIKES BACK

Visit us at www.abdopublishing.com

Reinforced library bound editions published in 2014 by Spotlight, a division of the ABDO Group, PO Box 398166, Minneapolis, MN 55439. Spotlight produces high-quality reinforced library bound editions for schools and libraries. Published by agreement with Marvel Characters, Inc.

Printed in the United States of America, Melrose Park, Illinois.
042013
092013
♻ This book contains at least 10% recycled material.

MARVEL

marvel.com
© 2013 Marvel

Library of Congress Cataloging-in-Publication Data

Caramagna, Joe.
 Iron Man and the armor wars / story by Joe Caramagna ; art by Craig Rousseau. -- Reinforced library edition.
      volumes cm
  Summary: "Cash, cars, boats, houses...Tony Stark has got it all. The only thing that could ruin his day? If every single one of his Iron Man armors were stolen, and then turned against him"-- Provided by publisher.
  ISBN 978-1-61479-164-5 (part 1: Down and out in Beverly Hills) --
  ISBN 978-1-61479-165-2 (part 2: The big red machine) --
  ISBN 978-1-61479-166-9 (part 3: How I learned to love the bomb) --
  ISBN 978-1-61479-167-6 (part 4: The Golden Avenger strikes back)
 1. Graphic novels. I. Rousseau, Craig, illustrator. II. Title.
PZ7.7.C3653Iro 2013
741.5'3--dc23
                                  2013003434

All Spotlight books are reinforced library bindings
and manufactured in the United States of America.

SOME PEOPLE SAY I'M A PLAYBOY.

THEY SAY IT LIKE IT'S A BAD THING, BUT I THINK IT'S A VIRTUE.

BECAUSE WHEN YOU HAVE ATTACHMENTS TO PEOPLE...

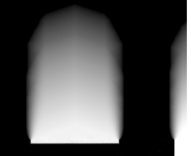

SPLASSH!

...YOU TEND TO LET YOUR GUARD DOWN.

CASE IN POINT: *JIM "RHODEY" RHODES.*

HE *USED* TO BE MY BEST FRIEND. BUT HE BETRAYED ME.

WELL, WELL, WELL. WELCOME TO OUR HUMBLE ABODE.

DEEP BELOW THE STREETS OF MANHATTAN...

RED BARBARIAN.

AREN'T THERE MORE OF YOU?

OMEGA RED GOT HUNGRY.

AND PLEASE ADDRESS ME BY MY RANK OF *GENERAL...*

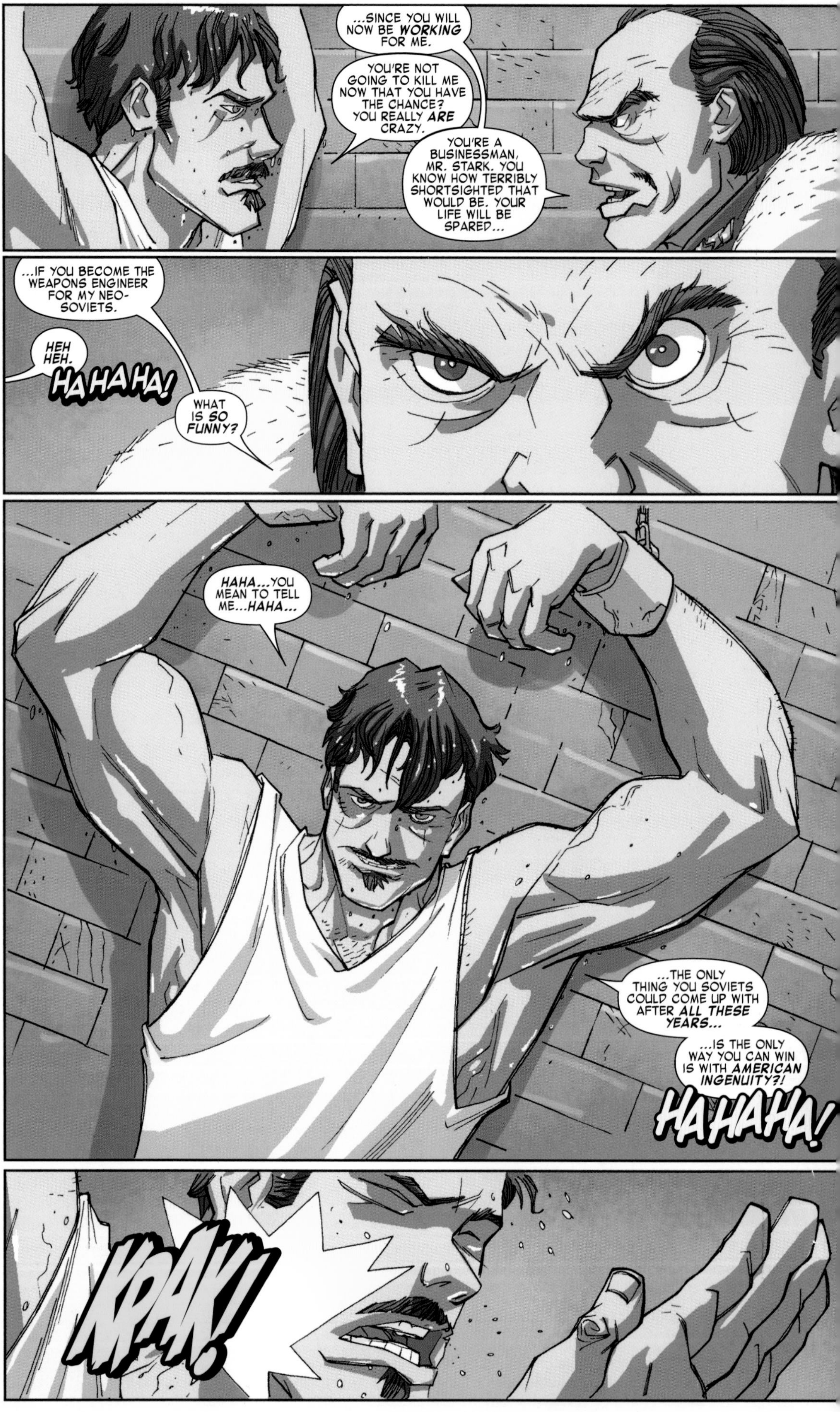
...SINCE YOU WILL NOW BE WORKING FOR ME.
YOU'RE NOT GOING TO KILL ME NOW THAT YOU HAVE THE CHANCE? YOU REALLY ARE CRAZY.
YOU'RE A BUSINESSMAN, MR. STARK. YOU KNOW HOW TERRIBLY SHORTSIGHTED THAT WOULD BE. YOUR LIFE WILL BE SPARED...
...IF YOU BECOME THE WEAPONS ENGINEER FOR MY NEO-SOVIETS.
HEH HEH.
HAHAHA!
WHAT IS SO FUNNY?
HAHA...YOU MEAN TO TELL ME...HAHA...
...THE ONLY THING YOU SOVIETS COULD COME UP WITH AFTER ALL THESE YEARS...
...IS THE ONLY WAY YOU CAN WIN IS WITH AMERICAN INGENUITY?!
HAHAHA!
KRAK!

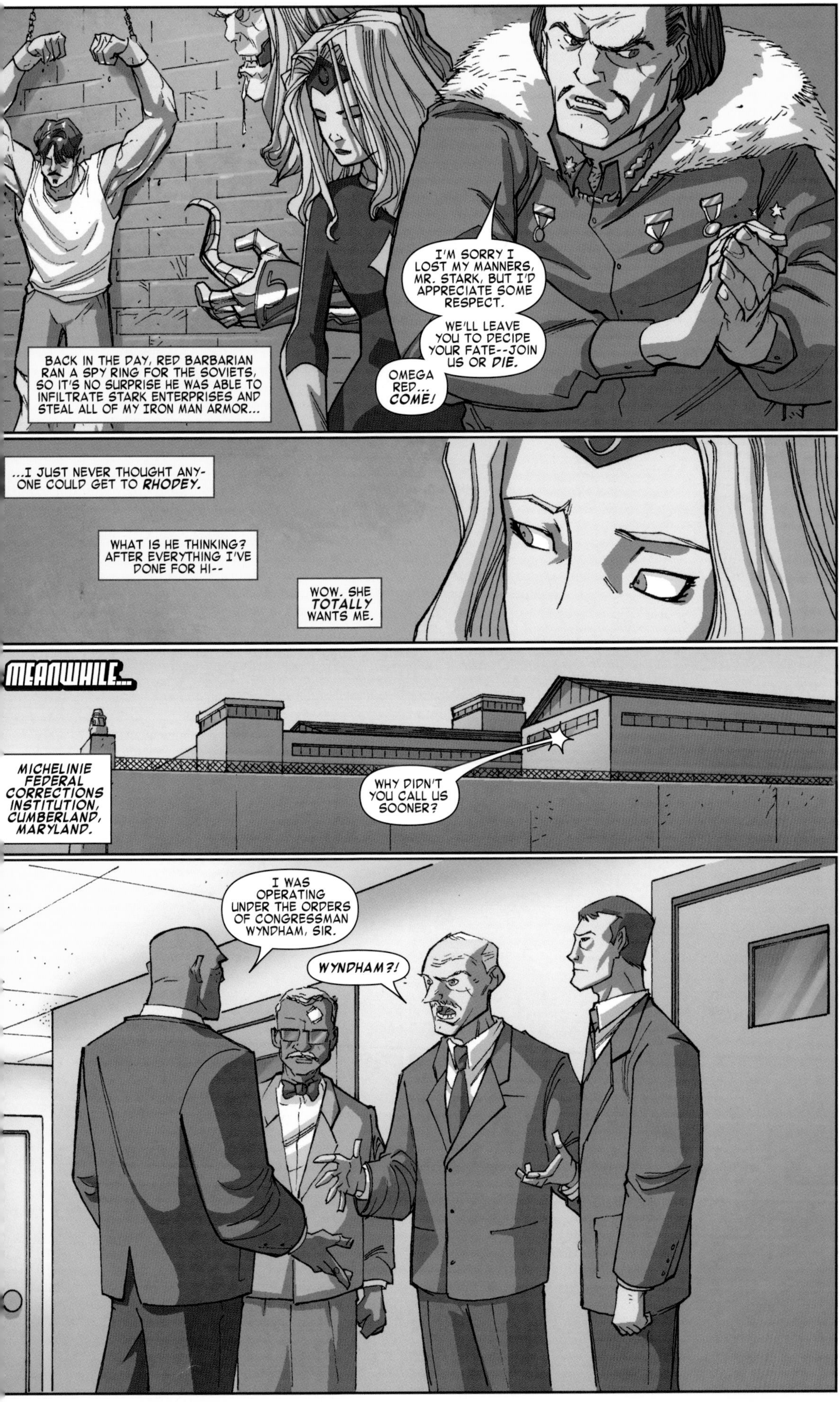

I'M SORRY I LOST MY MANNERS, MR. STARK, BUT I'D APPRECIATE SOME RESPECT.
WE'LL LEAVE YOU TO DECIDE YOUR FATE--JOIN US OR DIE.
OMEGA RED... COME!
BACK IN THE DAY, RED BARBARIAN RAN A SPY RING FOR THE SOVIETS, SO IT'S NO SURPRISE HE WAS ABLE TO INFILTRATE STARK ENTERPRISES AND STEAL ALL OF MY IRON MAN ARMOR...
...I JUST NEVER THOUGHT ANY-ONE COULD GET TO RHODEY.
WHAT IS HE THINKING? AFTER EVERYTHING I'VE DONE FOR HI--
WOW. SHE TOTALLY WANTS ME.
MEANWHILE...
MICHELINIE FEDERAL CORRECTIONS INSTITUTION, CUMBERLAND, MARYLAND.
WHY DIDN'T YOU CALL US SOONER?
I WAS OPERATING UNDER THE ORDERS OF CONGRESSMAN WYNDHAM, SIR.
WYNDHAM?!

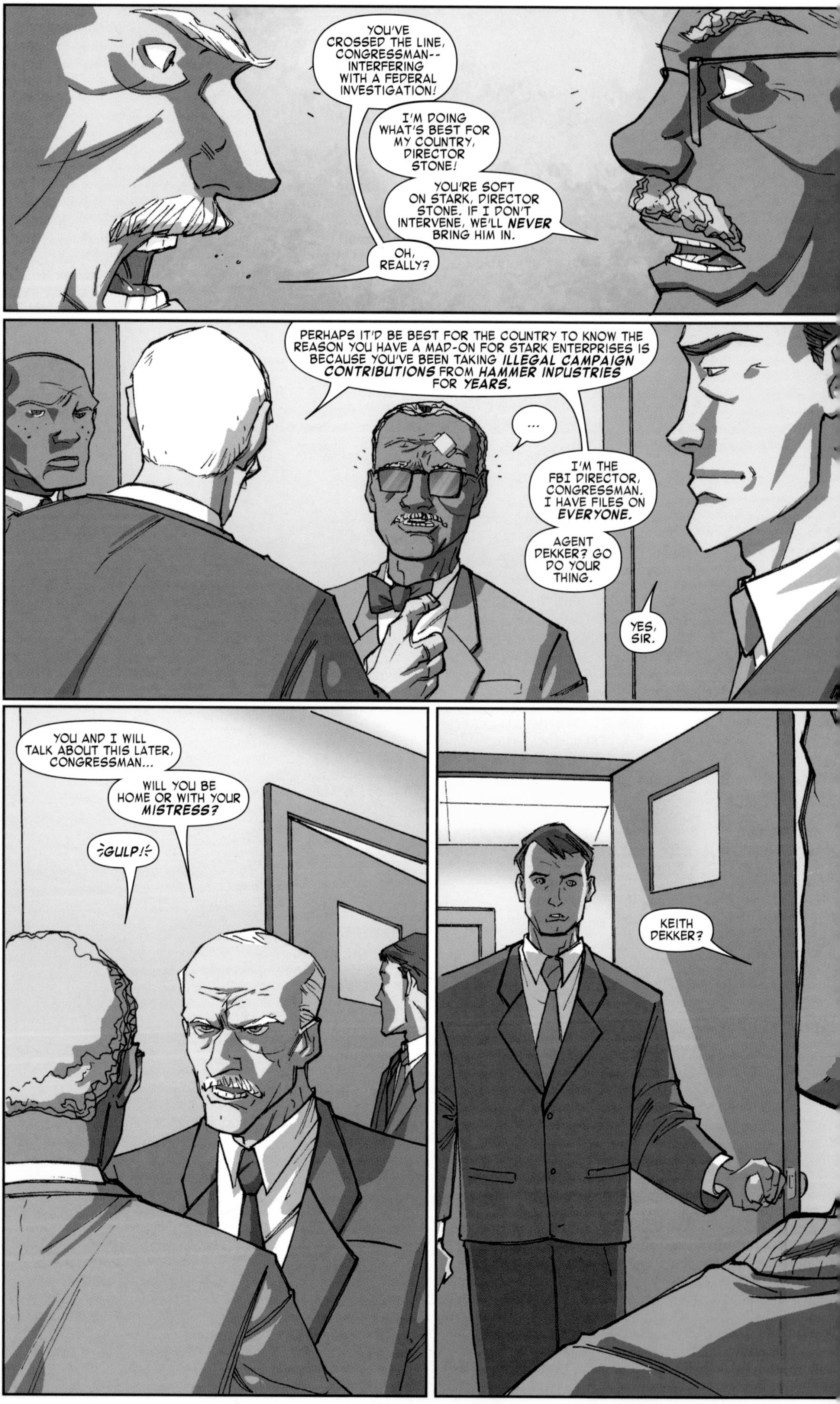
YOU'VE CROSSED THE LINE, CONGRESSMAN-- INTERFERING WITH A FEDERAL INVESTIGATION!
I'M DOING WHAT'S BEST FOR MY COUNTRY, DIRECTOR STONE!
YOU'RE SOFT ON STARK, DIRECTOR STONE. IF I DON'T INTERVENE, WE'LL *NEVER* BRING HIM IN.
OH, REALLY?
PERHAPS IT'D BE BEST FOR THE COUNTRY TO KNOW THE REASON YOU HAVE A MAD-ON FOR STARK ENTERPRISES IS BECAUSE YOU'VE BEEN TAKING *ILLEGAL CAMPAIGN CONTRIBUTIONS* FROM *HAMMER INDUSTRIES* FOR *YEARS.*
...
I'M THE FBI DIRECTOR, CONGRESSMAN. I HAVE FILES ON *EVERYONE.*
AGENT DEKKER? GO DO YOUR THING.
YES, SIR.
YOU AND I WILL TALK ABOUT THIS LATER, CONGRESSMAN...
WILL YOU BE HOME OR WITH YOUR *MISTRESS?*
GULP!
KEITH DEKKER?

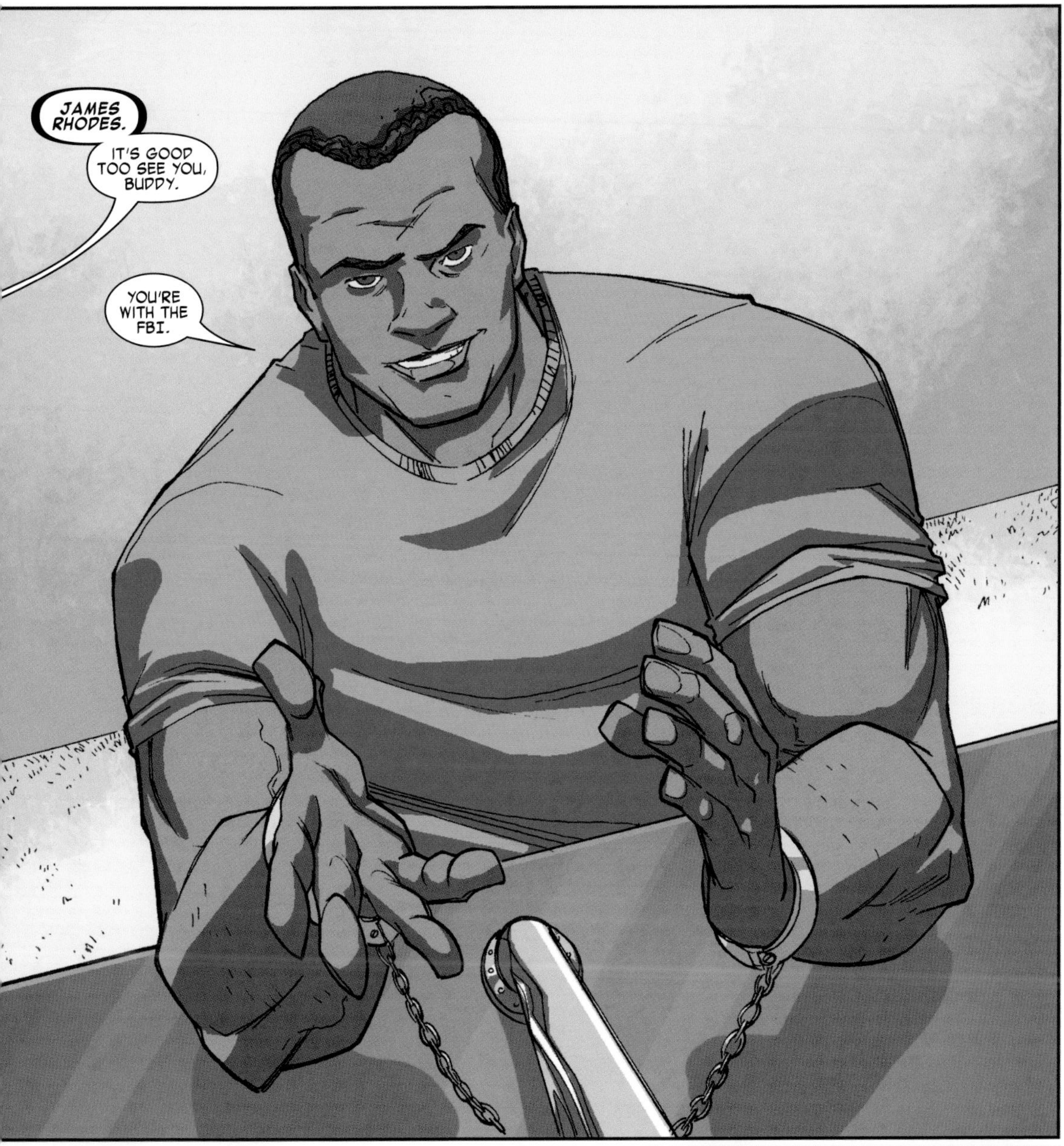
JAMES RHODES.
IT'S GOOD TOO SEE YOU, BUDDY.
YOU'RE WITH THE FBI.

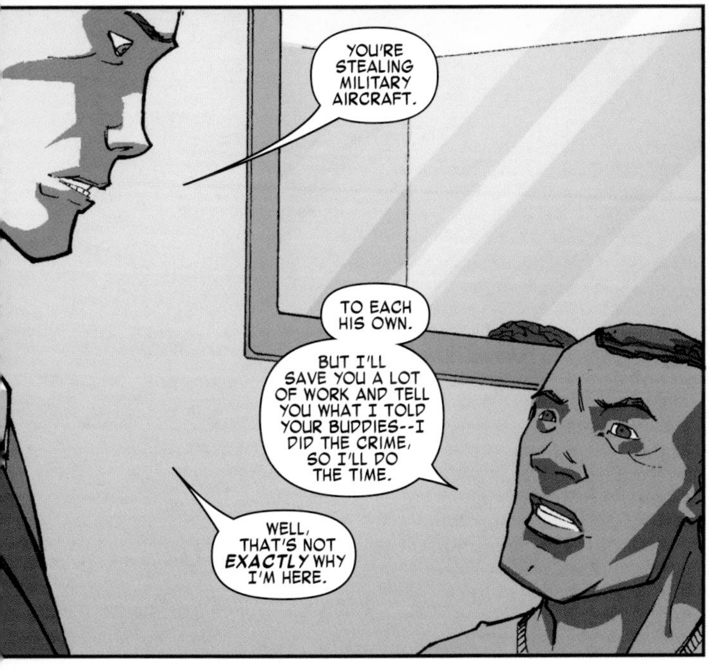
YOU'RE STEALING MILITARY AIRCRAFT.
TO EACH HIS OWN.
BUT I'LL SAVE YOU A LOT OF WORK AND TELL YOU WHAT I TOLD YOUR BUDDIES--I DID THE CRIME, SO I'LL DO THE TIME.
WELL, THAT'S NOT *EXACTLY* WHY I'M HERE.

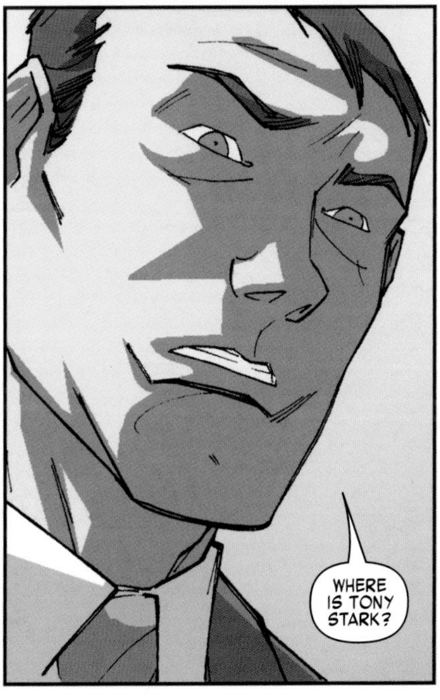
WHERE IS TONY STARK?

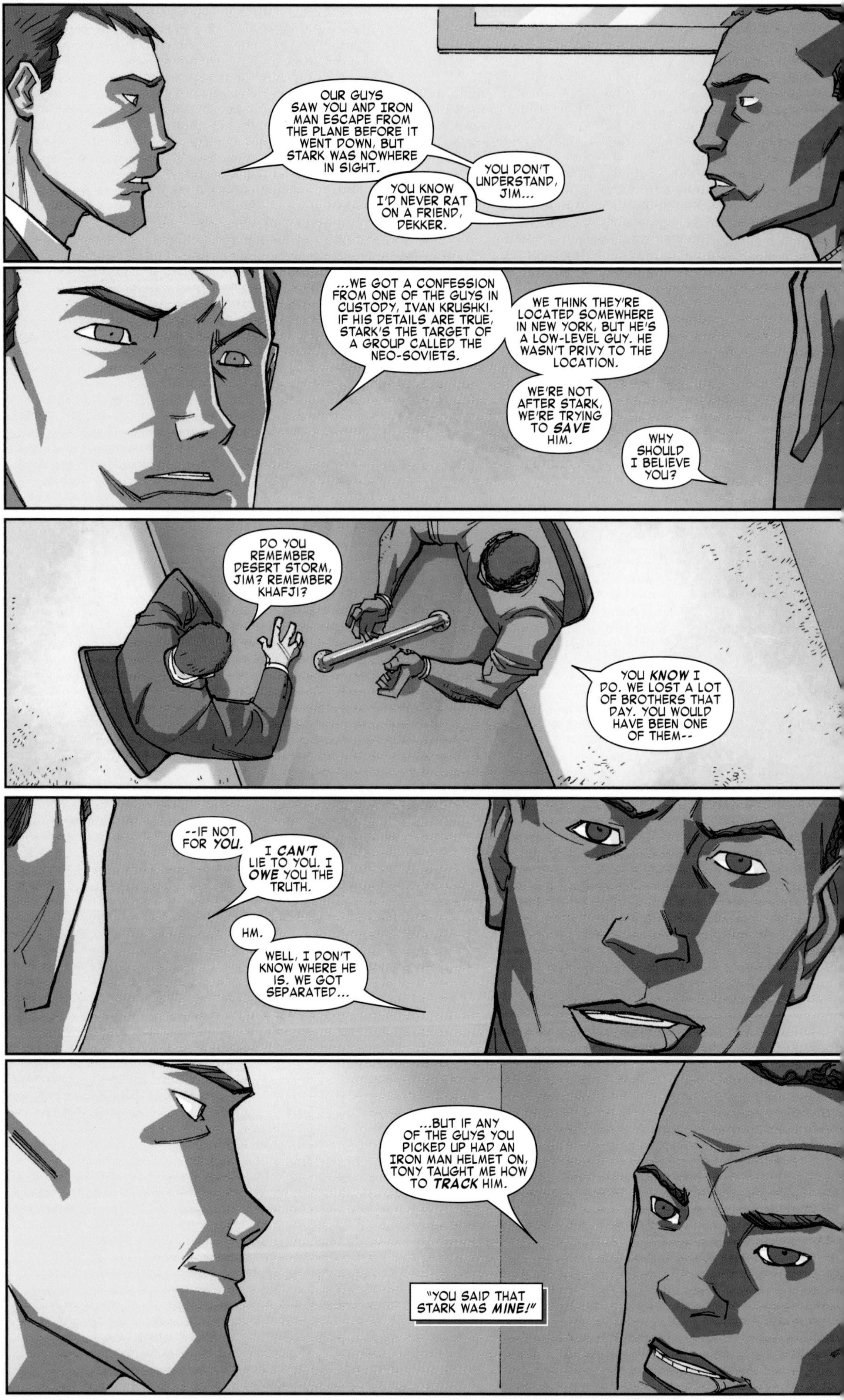
OUR GUYS SAW YOU AND IRON MAN ESCAPE FROM THE PLANE BEFORE IT WENT DOWN, BUT STARK WAS NOWHERE IN SIGHT.
YOU KNOW I'D NEVER RAT ON A FRIEND, DEKKER.
YOU DON'T UNDERSTAND, JIM...
...WE GOT A CONFESSION FROM ONE OF THE GUYS IN CUSTODY, IVAN KRUSHKI. IF HIS DETAILS ARE TRUE, STARK'S THE TARGET OF A GROUP CALLED THE NEO-SOVIETS.
WE THINK THEY'RE LOCATED SOMEWHERE IN NEW YORK, BUT HE'S A LOW-LEVEL GUY. HE WASN'T PRIVY TO THE LOCATION.
WE'RE NOT AFTER STARK, WE'RE TRYING TO SAVE HIM.
WHY SHOULD I BELIEVE YOU?
DO YOU REMEMBER DESERT STORM, JIM? REMEMBER KHAFJI?
YOU KNOW I DO. WE LOST A LOT OF BROTHERS THAT DAY. YOU WOULD HAVE BEEN ONE OF THEM--
--IF NOT FOR YOU.
I CAN'T LIE TO YOU. I OWE YOU THE TRUTH.
HM.
WELL, I DON'T KNOW WHERE HE IS. WE GOT SEPARATED...
...BUT IF ANY OF THE GUYS YOU PICKED UP HAD AN IRON MAN HELMET ON, TONY TAUGHT ME HOW TO TRACK HIM.
"YOU SAID THAT STARK WAS MINE!"

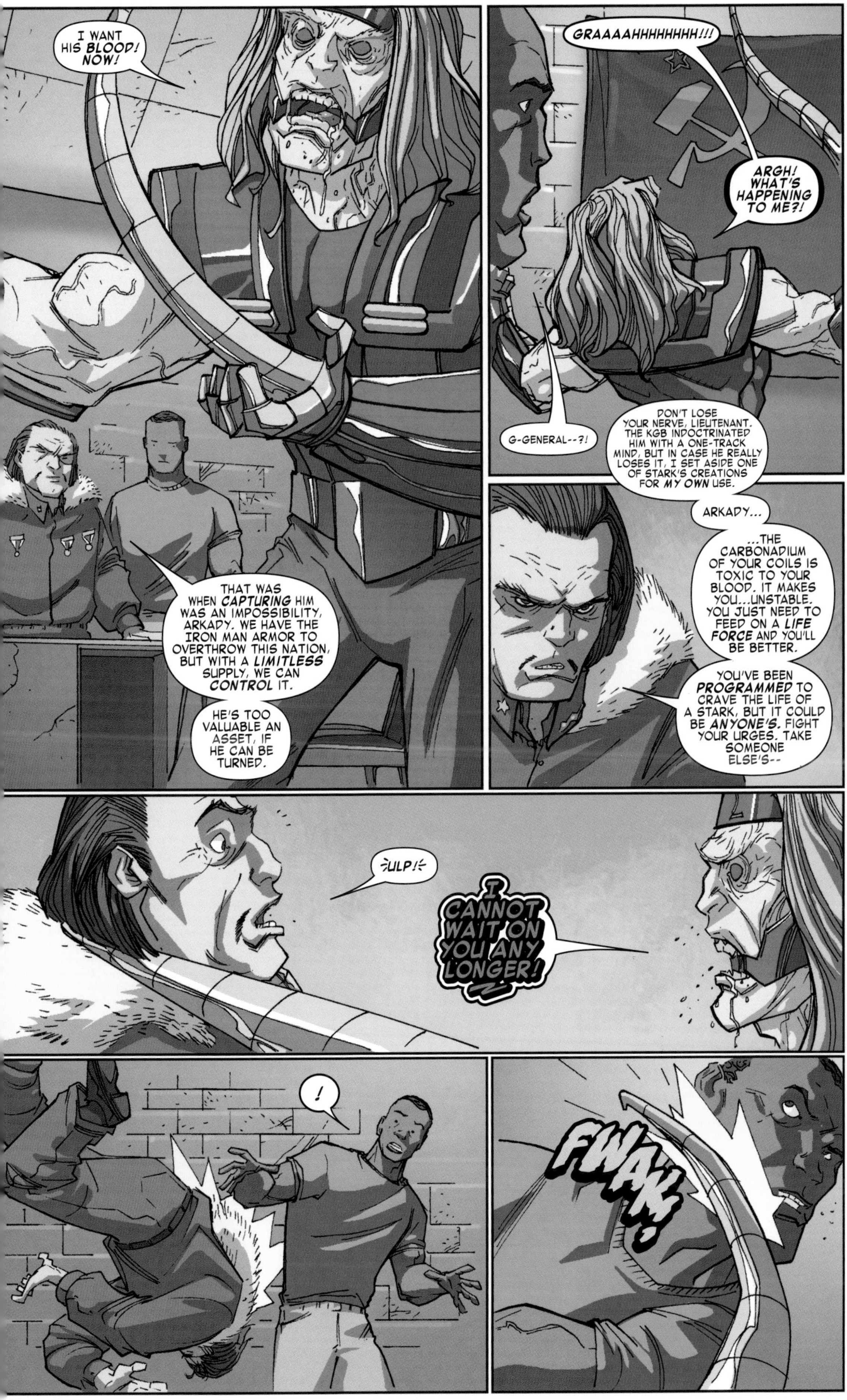
I WANT HIS BLOOD! NOW!
THAT WAS WHEN CAPTURING HIM WAS AN IMPOSSIBILITY, ARKADY. WE HAVE THE IRON MAN ARMOR TO OVERTHROW THIS NATION, BUT WITH A LIMITLESS SUPPLY, WE CAN CONTROL IT.
HE'S TOO VALUABLE AN ASSET, IF HE CAN BE TURNED.
GRAAAAAHHHHHHHH!!!
ARGH! WHAT'S HAPPENING TO ME?!
G-GENERAL--?!
DON'T LOSE YOUR NERVE, LIEUTENANT. THE KGB INDOCTRINATED HIM WITH A ONE-TRACK MIND, BUT IN CASE HE REALLY LOSES IT, I SET ASIDE ONE OF STARK'S CREATIONS FOR MY OWN USE.
ARKADY...
...THE CARBONADIUM OF YOUR COILS IS TOXIC TO YOUR BLOOD. IT MAKES YOU...UNSTABLE. YOU JUST NEED TO FEED ON A LIFE FORCE AND YOU'LL BE BETTER.
YOU'VE BEEN PROGRAMMED TO CRAVE THE LIFE OF A STARK, BUT IT COULD BE ANYONE'S. FIGHT YOUR URGES. TAKE SOMEONE ELSE'S--
ULP!
I CANNOT WAIT ON YOU ANY LONGER!
!
FWAK!

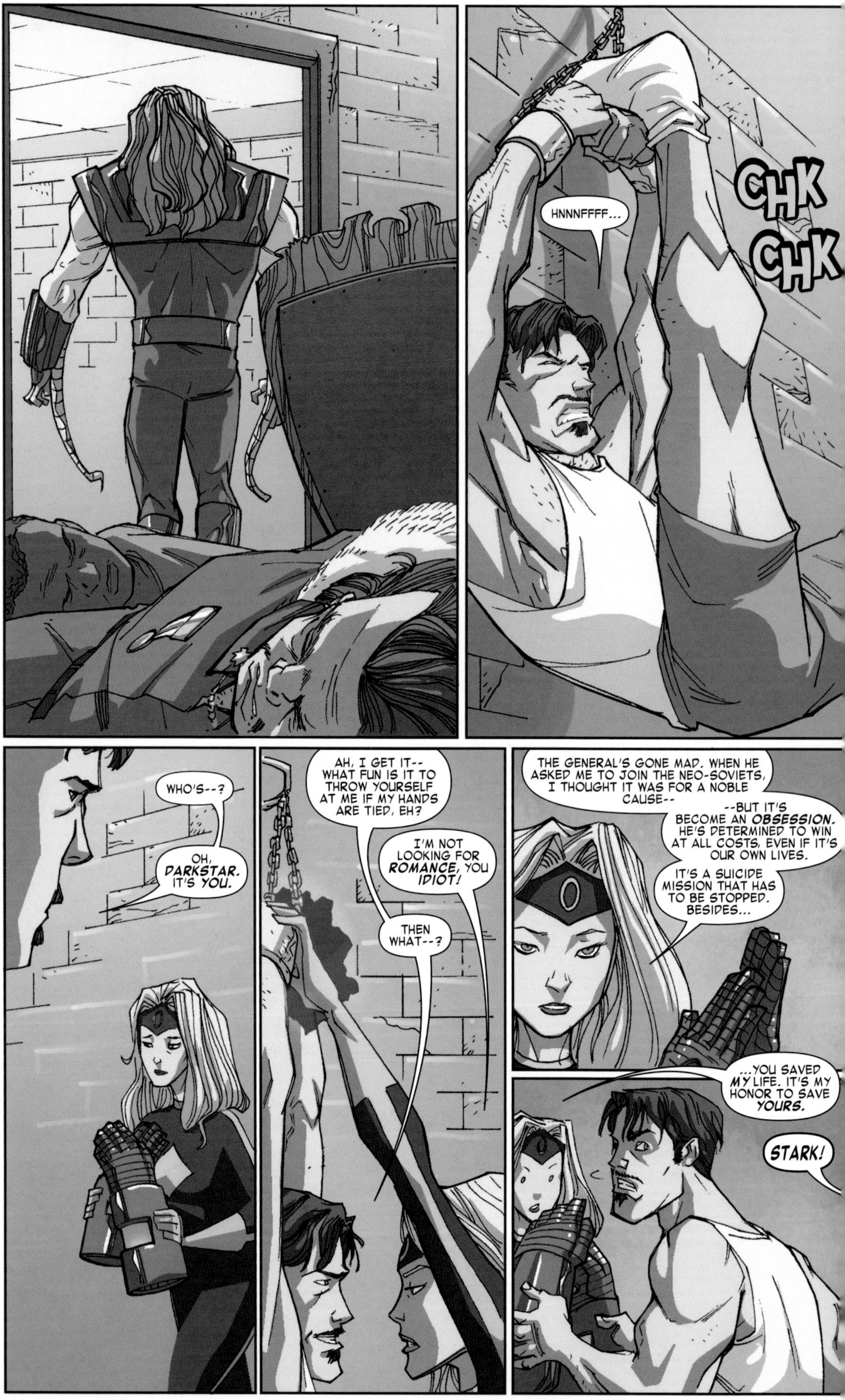
HNNNFFFF...
CHK
CHK
WHO'S--?
OH, DARKSTAR. IT'S YOU.
AH, I GET IT-- WHAT FUN IS IT TO THROW YOURSELF AT ME IF MY HANDS ARE TIED, EH?
I'M NOT LOOKING FOR ROMANCE, YOU IDIOT!
THEN WHAT--?
THE GENERAL'S GONE MAD. WHEN HE ASKED ME TO JOIN THE NEO-SOVIETS, I THOUGHT IT WAS FOR A NOBLE CAUSE--
--BUT IT'S BECOME AN OBSESSION. HE'S DETERMINED TO WIN AT ALL COSTS, EVEN IF IT'S OUR OWN LIVES.
IT'S A SUICIDE MISSION THAT HAS TO BE STOPPED. BESIDES...
...YOU SAVED MY LIFE. IT'S MY HONOR TO SAVE YOURS.
STARK!

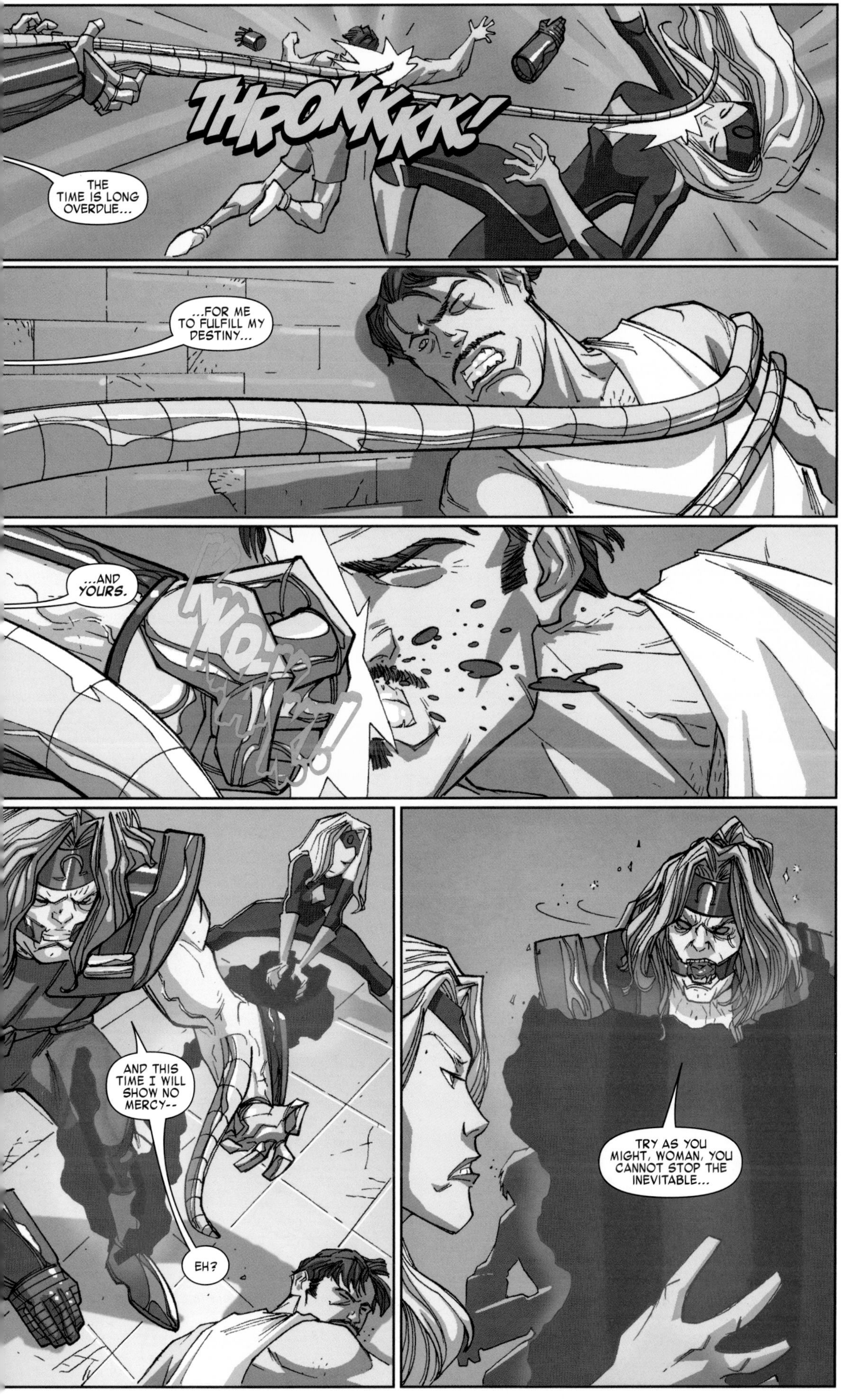
THROKKKK!
THE TIME IS LONG OVERDUE...
...FOR ME TO FULFILL MY DESTINY...
...AND *YOURS.*
AND THIS TIME I WILL SHOW NO MERCY--
EH?
TRY AS YOU MIGHT, WOMAN, YOU CANNOT STOP THE INEVITABLE...

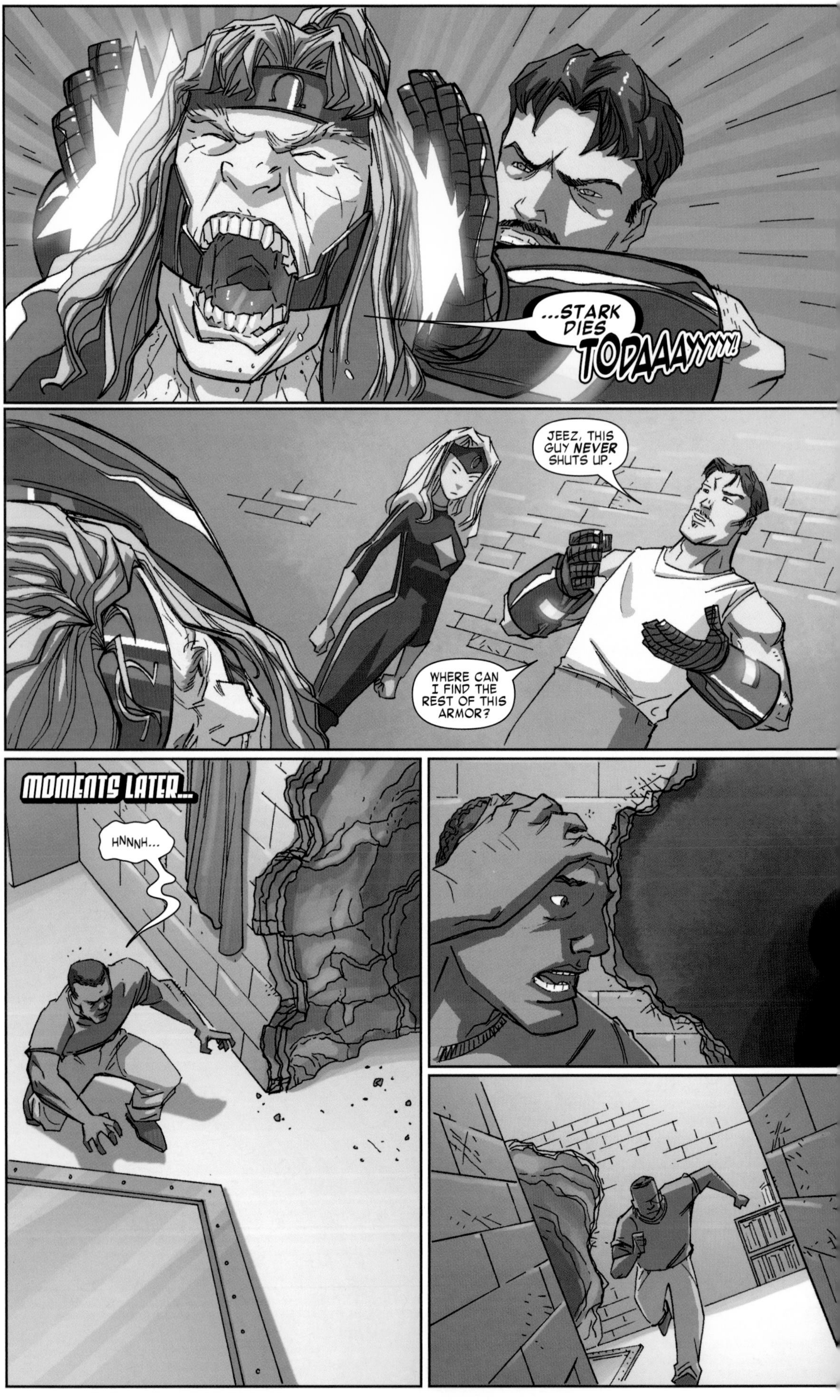
...STARK DIES TODAAAYYYYY!
JEEZ, THIS GUY NEVER SHUTS UP.
WHERE CAN I FIND THE REST OF THIS ARMOR?
MOMENTS LATER...
HNNNH...

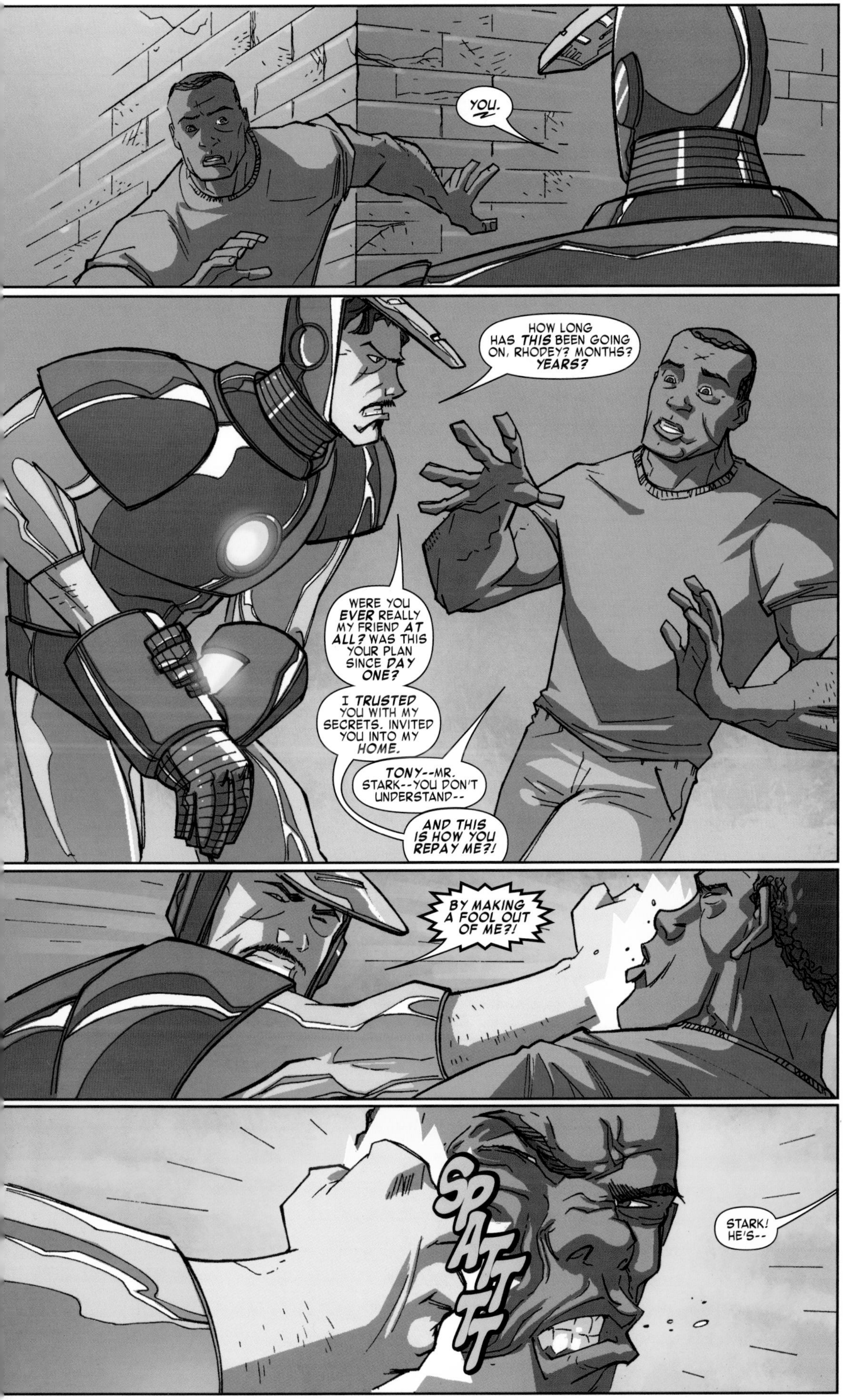

YOU.
HOW LONG HAS THIS BEEN GOING ON, RHODEY? MONTHS? YEARS?
WERE YOU EVER REALLY MY FRIEND AT ALL? WAS THIS YOUR PLAN SINCE DAY ONE?
I TRUSTED YOU WITH MY SECRETS. INVITED YOU INTO MY HOME.
TONY--MR. STARK--YOU DON'T UNDERSTAND--
AND THIS IS HOW YOU REPAY ME?!
BY MAKING A FOOL OUT OF ME?!
SPATTT
STARK! HE'S--

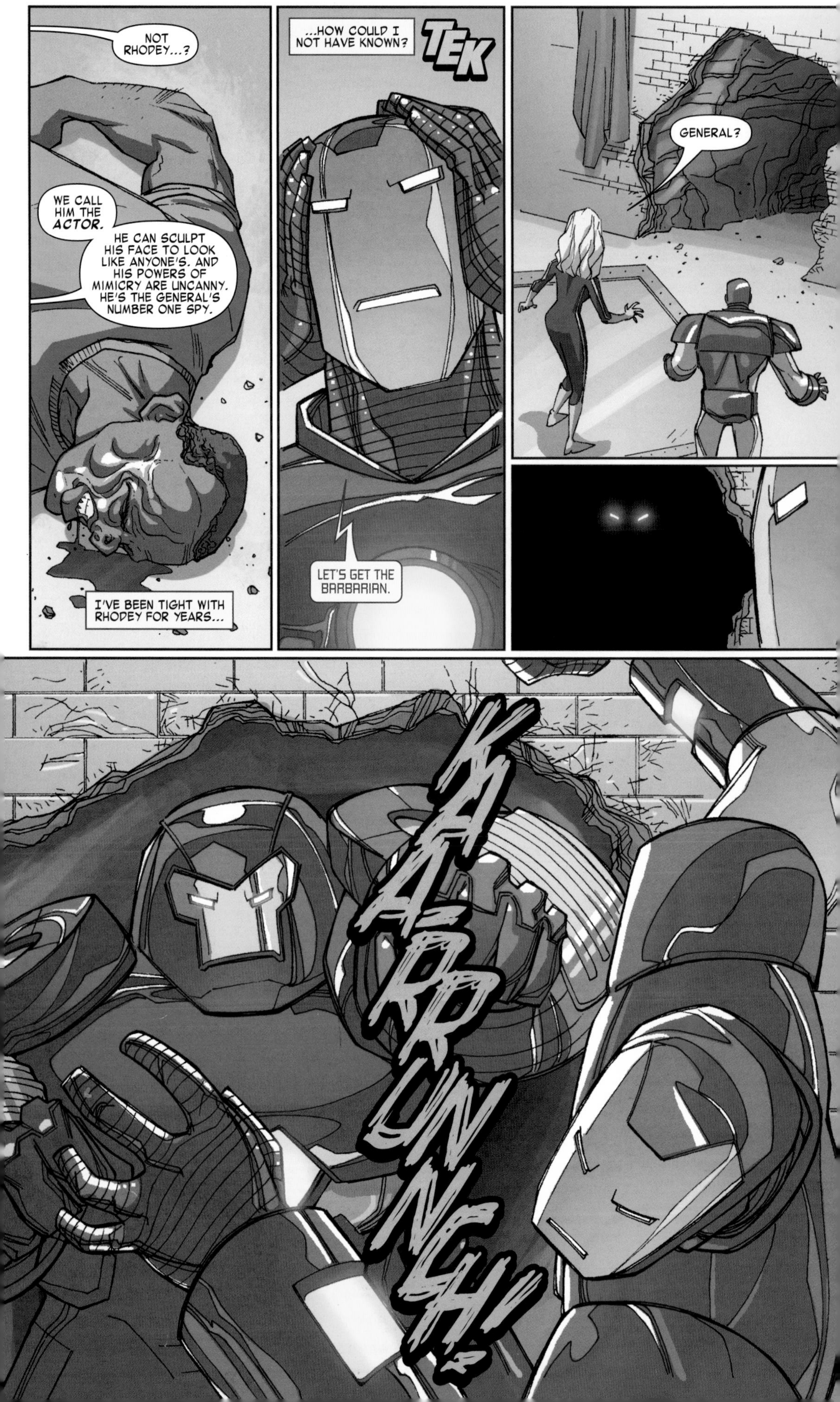
NOT RHODEY...?
WE CALL HIM THE ACTOR.
HE CAN SCULPT HIS FACE TO LOOK LIKE ANYONE'S. AND HIS POWERS OF MIMICRY ARE UNCANNY. HE'S THE GENERAL'S NUMBER ONE SPY.
I'VE BEEN TIGHT WITH RHODEY FOR YEARS...
...HOW COULD I NOT HAVE KNOWN?
TEK
LET'S GET THE BARBARIAN.
GENERAL?
KRARRUNNCH!

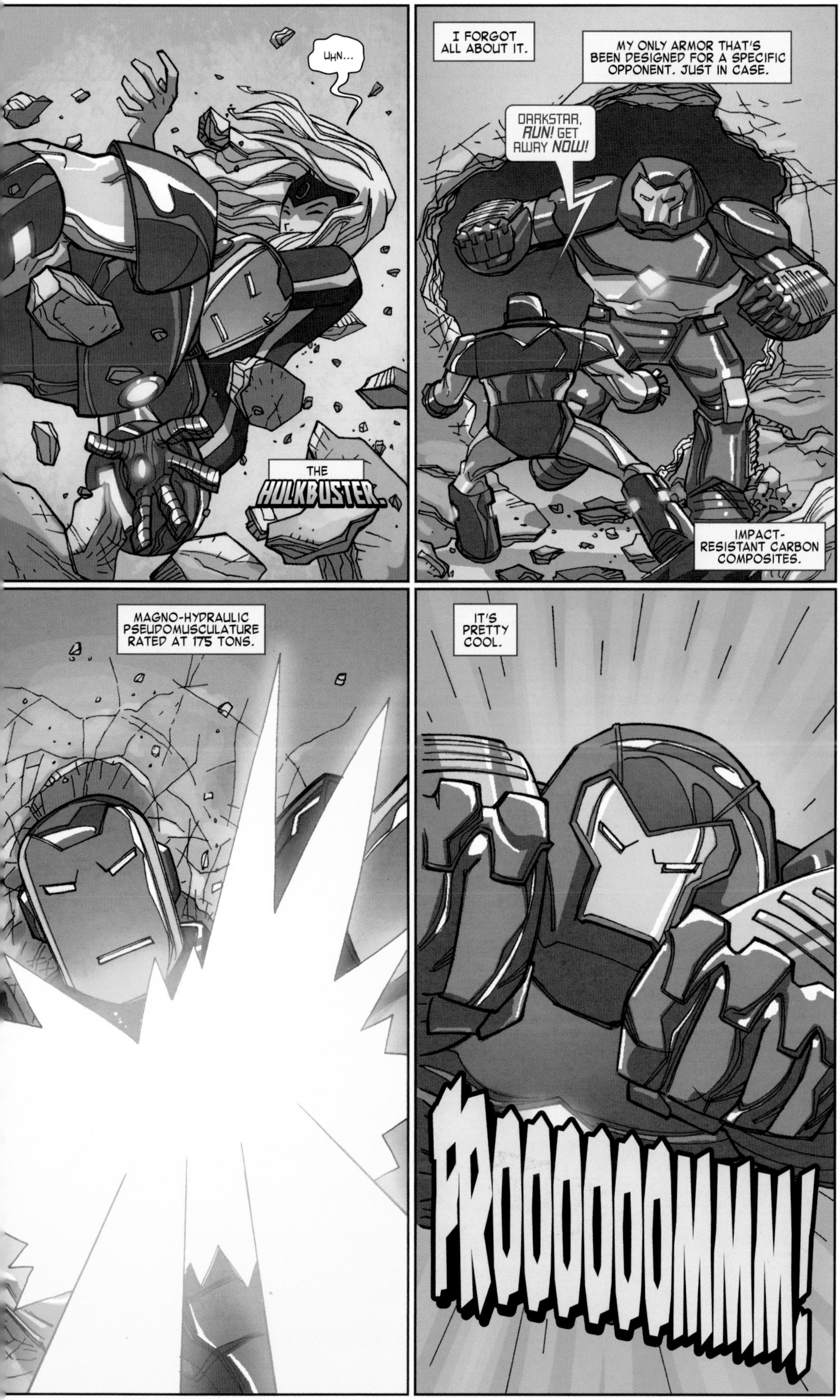
UHN...
THE
HULKBUSTER.
I FORGOT ALL ABOUT IT.
MY ONLY ARMOR THAT'S BEEN DESIGNED FOR A SPECIFIC OPPONENT. JUST IN CASE.
DARKSTAR, RUN! GET AWAY NOW!
IMPACT-RESISTANT CARBON COMPOSITES.
MAGNO-HYDRAULIC PSEUDOMUSCULATURE RATED AT 175 TONS.
IT'S PRETTY COOL.
PROOOOOOMMM!

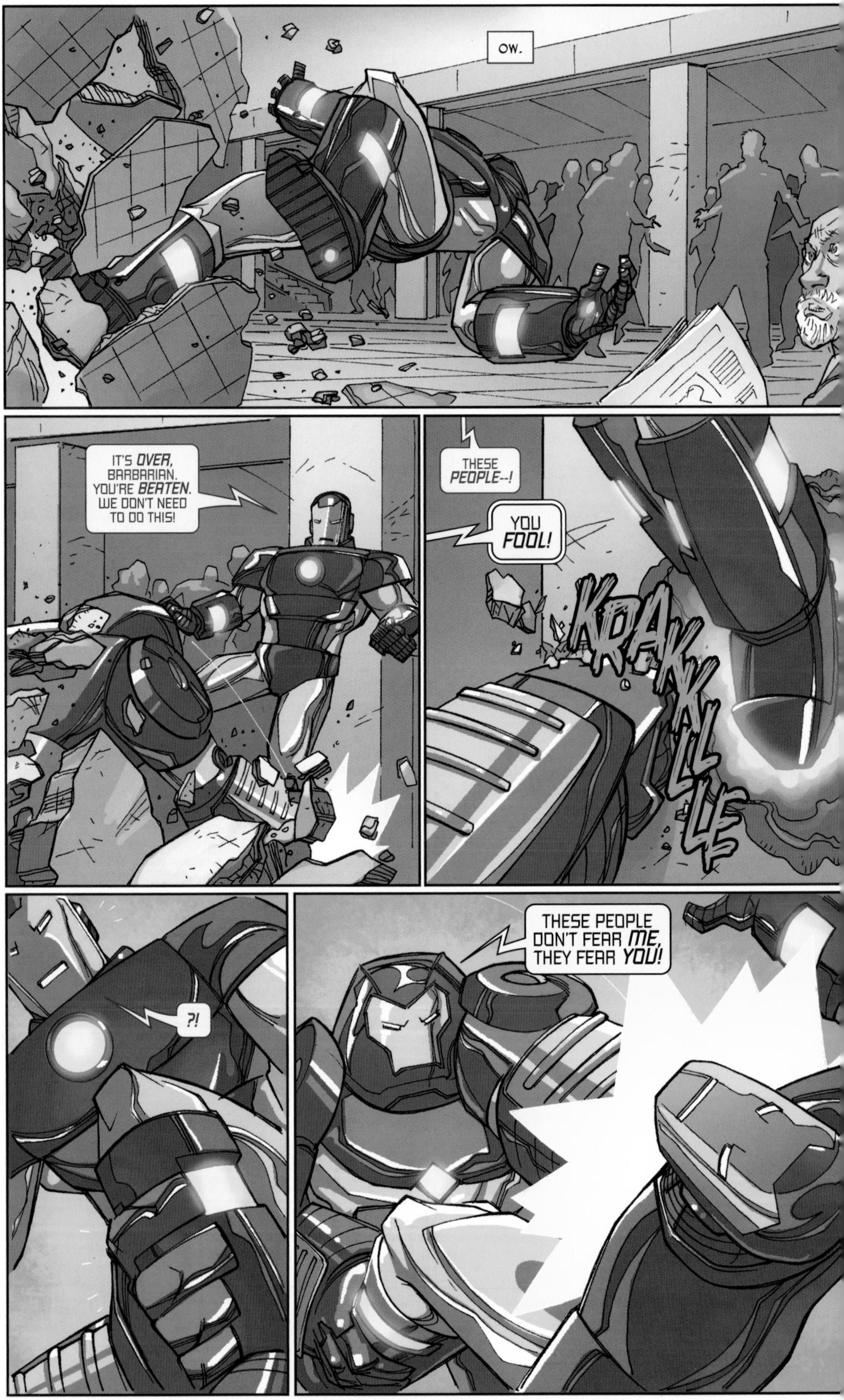
OW.
IT'S *OVER*, BARBARIAN. YOU'RE *BEATEN*. WE DON'T NEED TO DO THIS!
THESE *PEOPLE*--!
YOU *FOOL!*
KRAKKLLE
?!
THESE PEOPLE DON'T FEAR *ME*, THEY FEAR *YOU!*

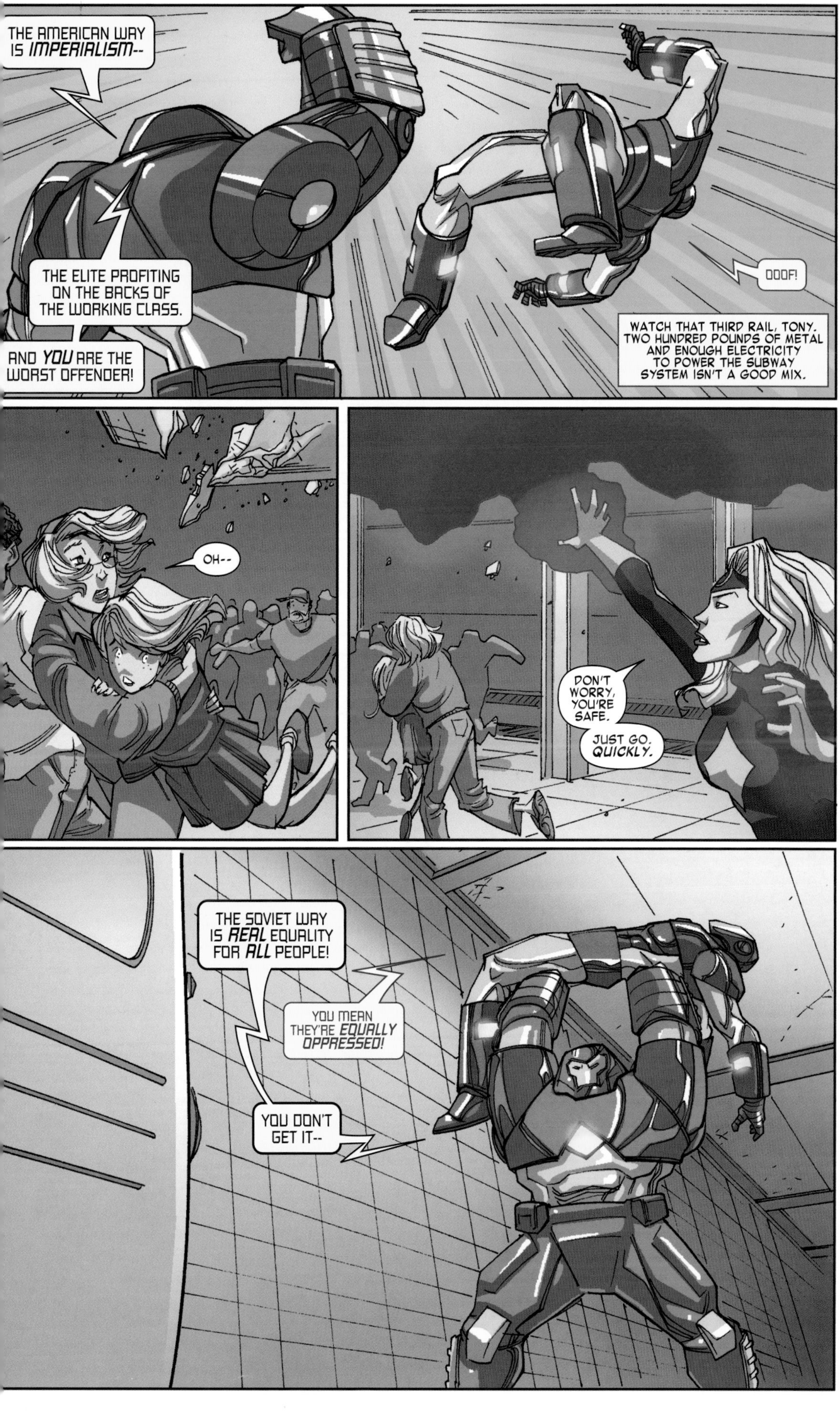
THE AMERICAN WAY IS IMPERIALISM--
THE ELITE PROFITING ON THE BACKS OF THE WORKING CLASS.
AND YOU ARE THE WORST OFFENDER!
OOOF!
WATCH THAT THIRD RAIL, TONY. TWO HUNDRED POUNDS OF METAL AND ENOUGH ELECTRICITY TO POWER THE SUBWAY SYSTEM ISN'T A GOOD MIX.
OH--
DON'T WORRY, YOU'RE SAFE.
JUST GO. QUICKLY.
THE SOVIET WAY IS REAL EQUALITY FOR ALL PEOPLE!
YOU MEAN THEY'RE EQUALLY OPPRESSED!
YOU DON'T GET IT--

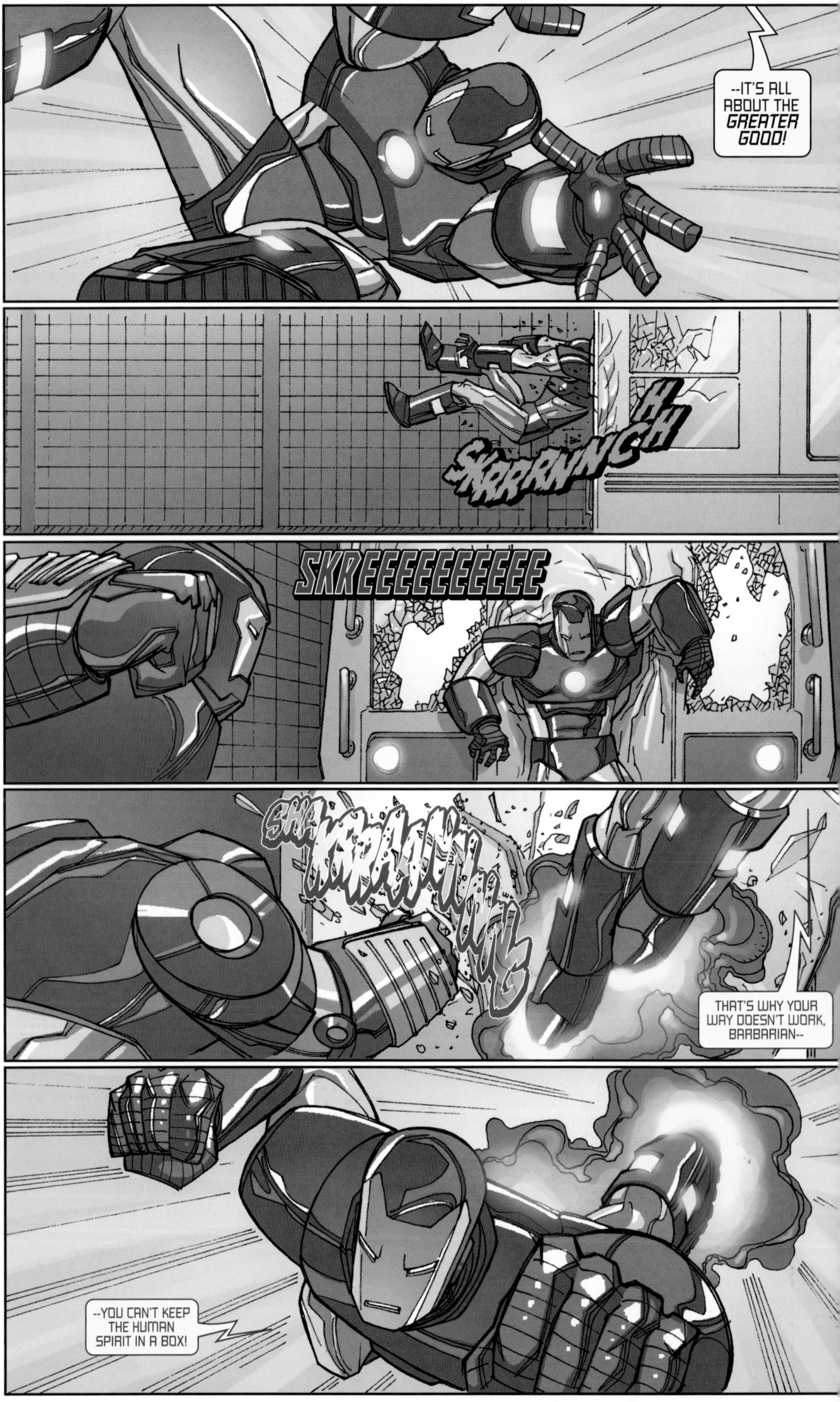
--IT'S ALL ABOUT THE *GREATER GOOD!*
THAT'S WHY YOUR WAY DOESN'T WORK, BARBARIAN--
--YOU CAN'T KEEP THE HUMAN SPIRIT IN A BOX!

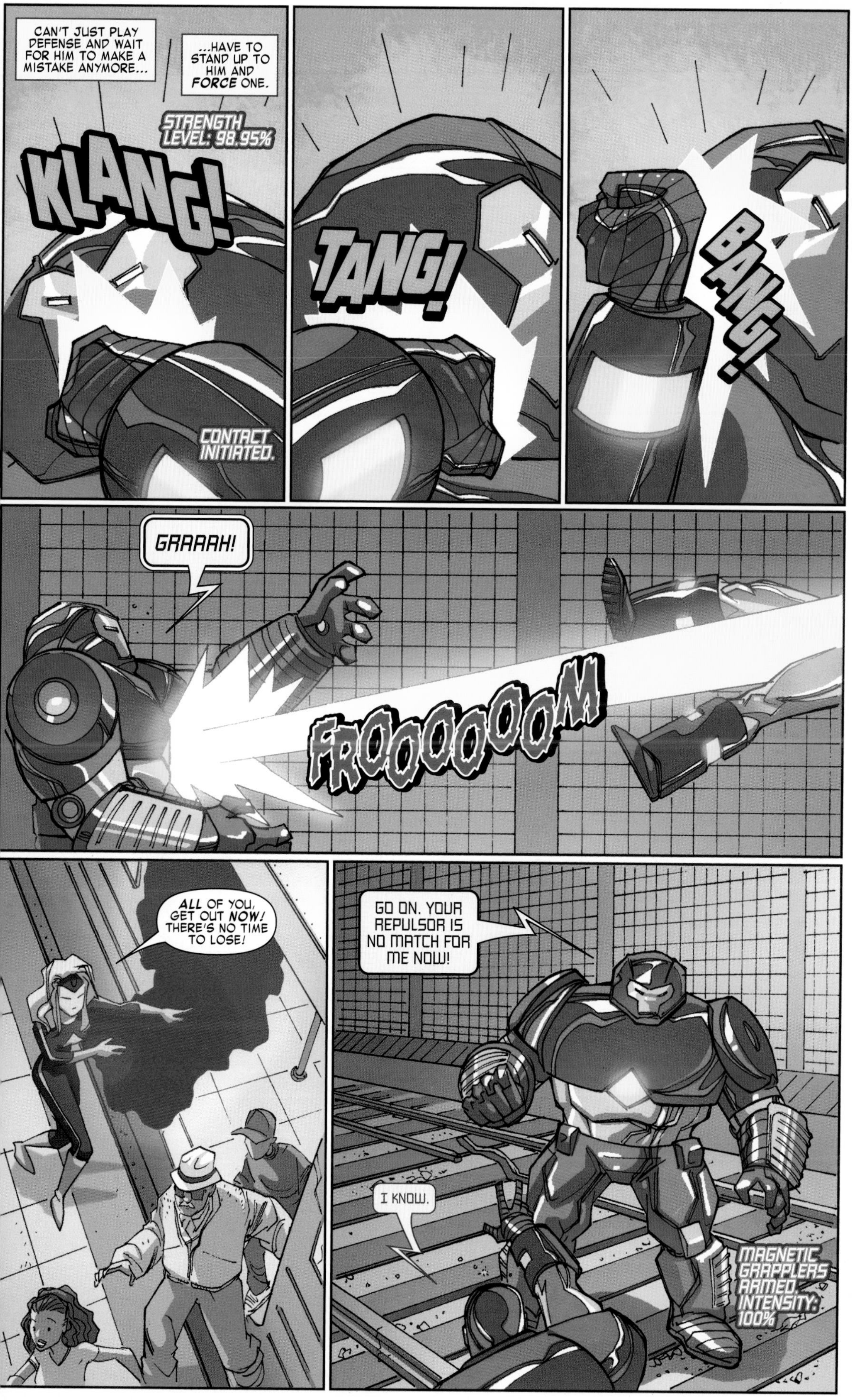
CAN'T JUST PLAY DEFENSE AND WAIT FOR HIM TO MAKE A MISTAKE ANYMORE...
...HAVE TO STAND UP TO HIM AND FORCE ONE.
STRENGTH LEVEL: 98.95%
KLANG!
CONTACT INITIATED.
TANG!
BANG!
GRAAAH!
FROOOOOOOM
ALL OF YOU, GET OUT NOW! THERE'S NO TIME TO LOSE!
GO ON. YOUR REPULSOR IS NO MATCH FOR ME NOW!
I KNOW.
MAGNETIC GRAPPLERS ARMED. INTENSITY: 100%

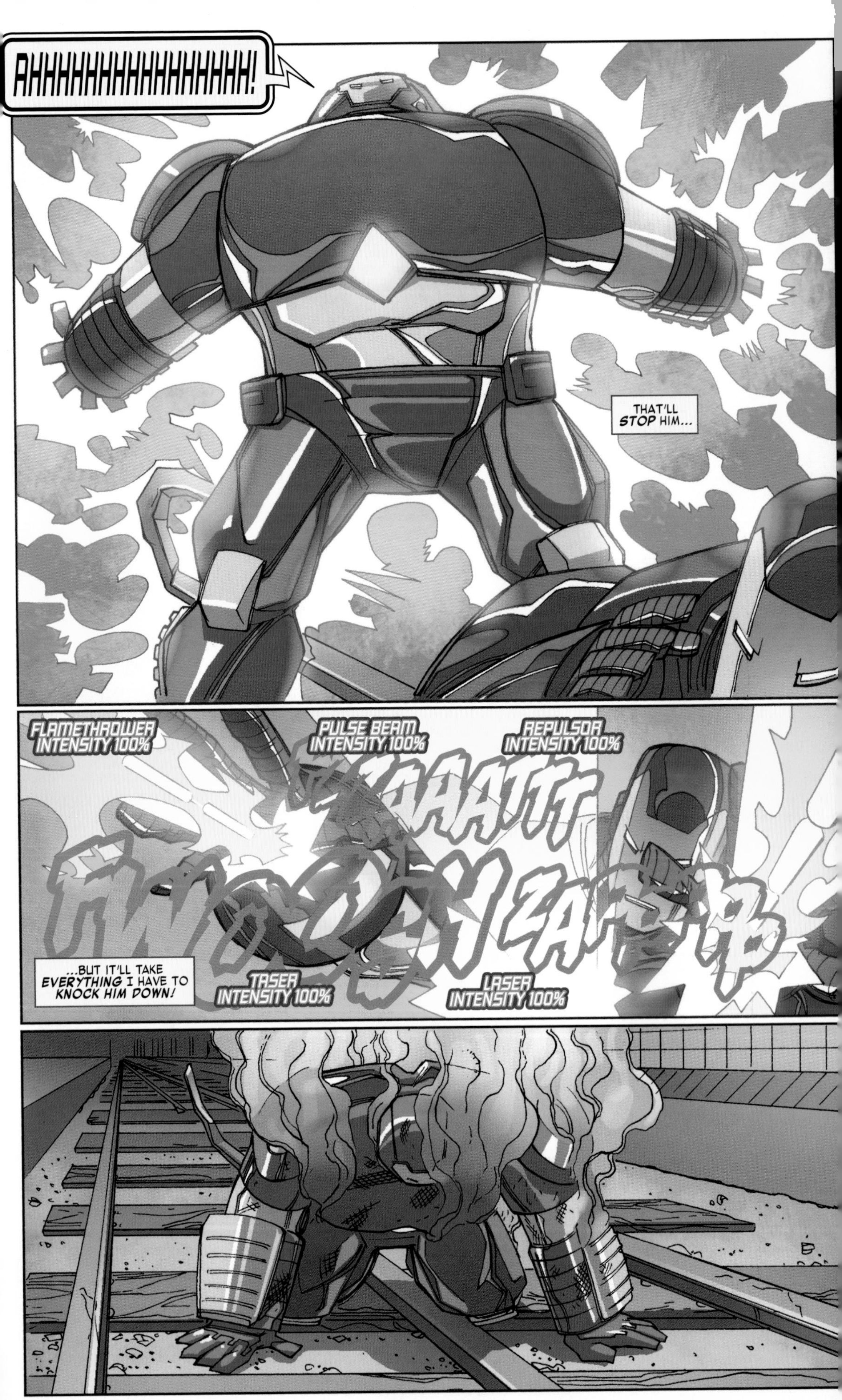
AHHHHHHHHHHHHHHH!
THAT'LL STOP HIM...
FLAMETHROWER INTENSITY 100%
PULSE BEAM INTENSITY 100%
REPULSOR INTENSITY 100%
...BUT IT'LL TAKE EVERYTHING I HAVE TO KNOCK HIM DOWN!
TASER INTENSITY 100%
LASER INTENSITY 100%

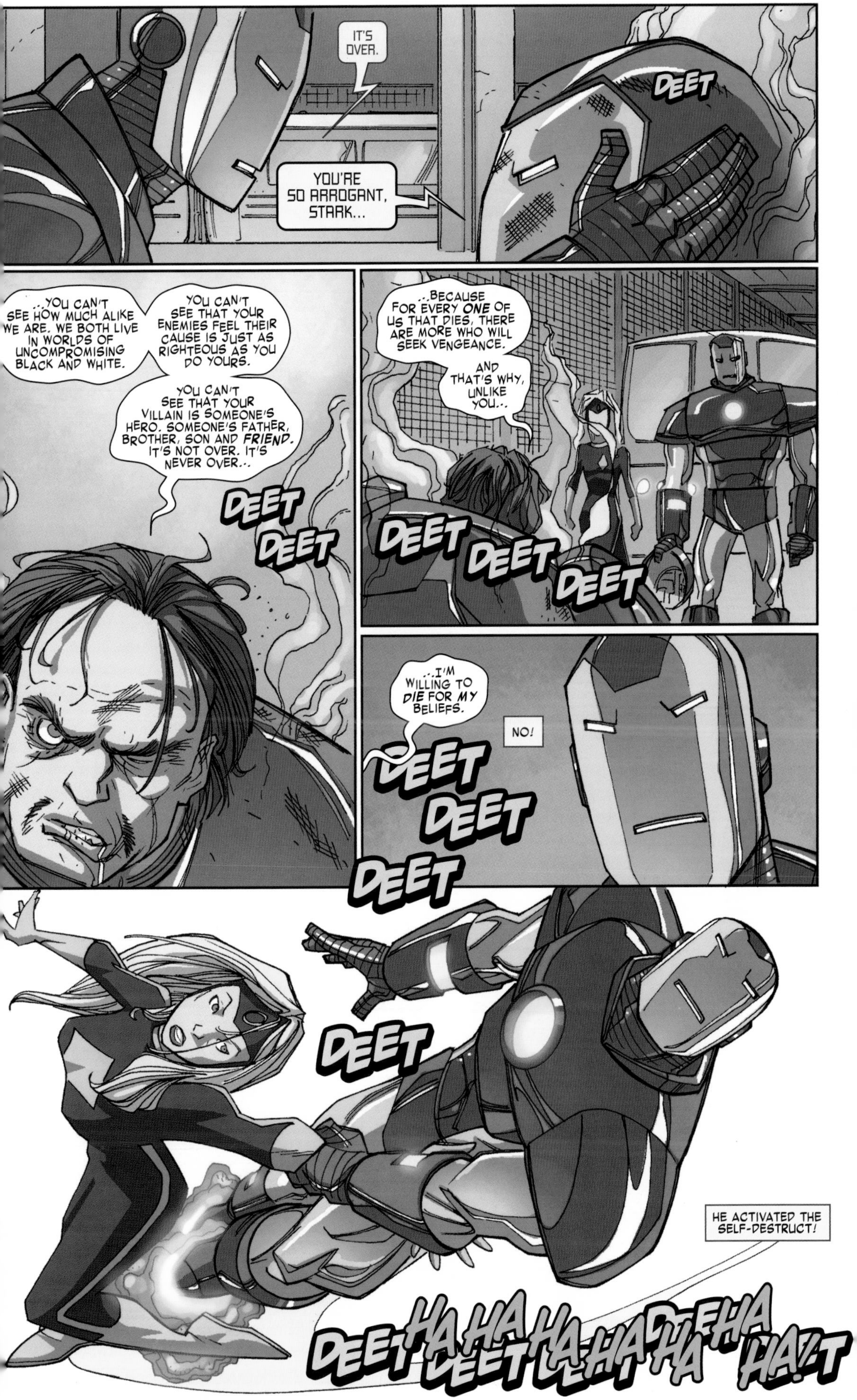
IT'S OVER.
DEET
YOU'RE SO ARROGANT, STARK...
...YOU CAN'T SEE HOW MUCH ALIKE WE ARE. WE BOTH LIVE IN WORLDS OF UNCOMPROMISING BLACK AND WHITE.
YOU CAN'T SEE THAT YOUR ENEMIES FEEL THEIR CAUSE IS JUST AS RIGHTEOUS AS YOU DO YOURS.
YOU CAN'T SEE THAT YOUR VILLAIN IS SOMEONE'S HERO. SOMEONE'S FATHER, BROTHER, SON AND FRIEND. IT'S NOT OVER. IT'S NEVER OVER...
DEET DEET
...BECAUSE FOR EVERY ONE OF US THAT DIES, THERE ARE MORE WHO WILL SEEK VENGEANCE.
AND THAT'S WHY, UNLIKE YOU...
DEET DEET DEET
...I'M WILLING TO DIE FOR MY BELIEFS.
NO!
DEET DEET DEET
DEET
HE ACTIVATED THE SELF-DESTRUCT!
DEET HA HA DEET HA HA HA HA HA

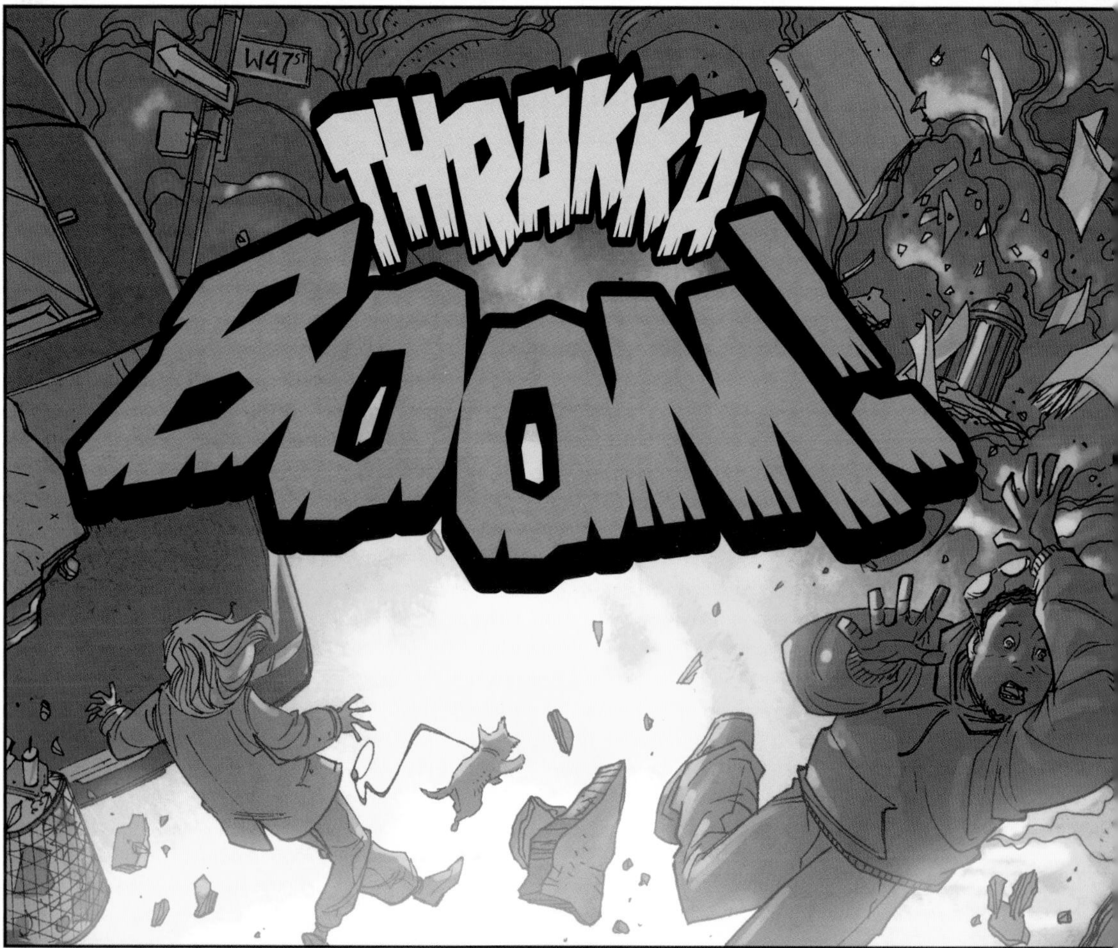
W47ST
THRAKKA BOOM!

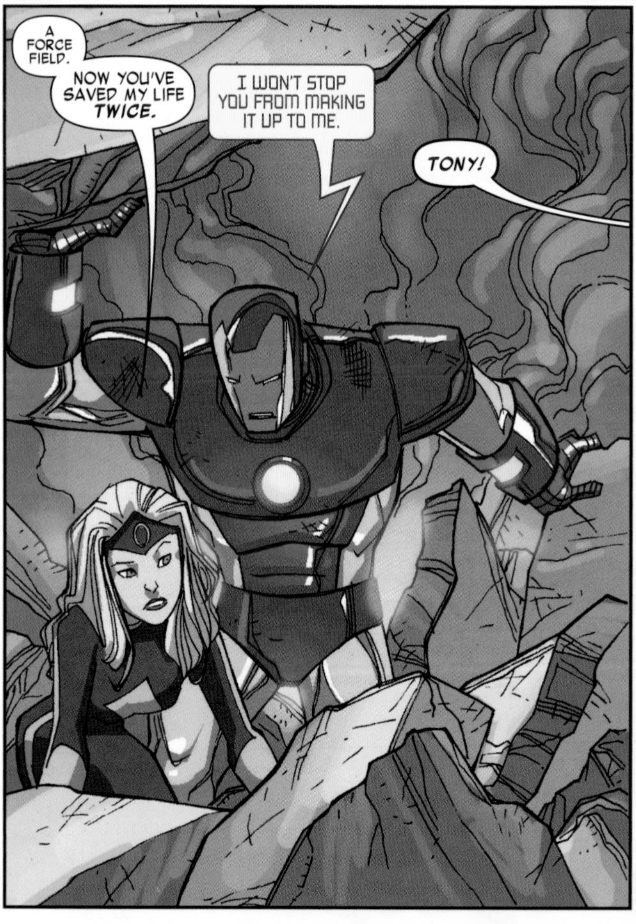
A FORCE FIELD.
NOW YOU'VE SAVED MY LIFE TWICE.
I WON'T STOP YOU FROM MAKING IT UP TO ME.
TONY!

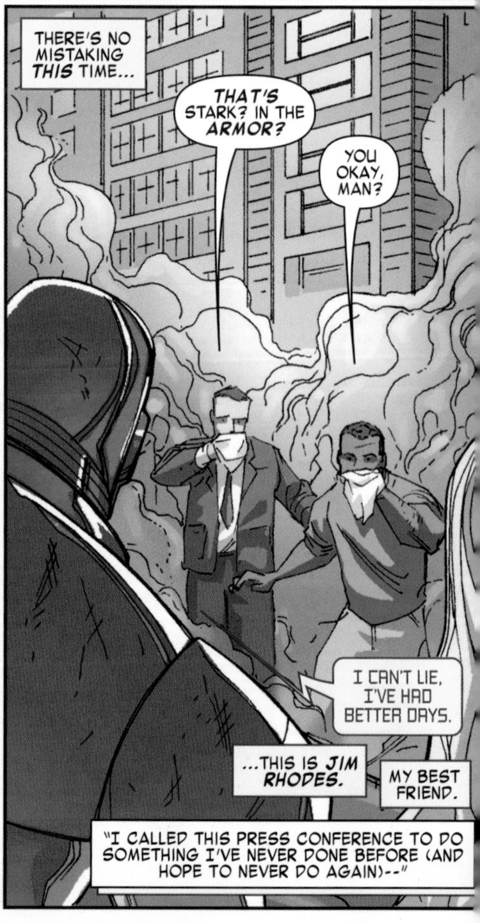
THERE'S NO MISTAKING THIS TIME...
THAT'S STARK? IN THE ARMOR?
YOU OKAY, MAN?
I CAN'T LIE, I'VE HAD BETTER DAYS.
...THIS IS JIM RHODES.
MY BEST FRIEND.
"I CALLED THIS PRESS CONFERENCE TO DO SOMETHING I'VE NEVER DONE BEFORE (AND HOPE TO NEVER DO AGAIN)--"

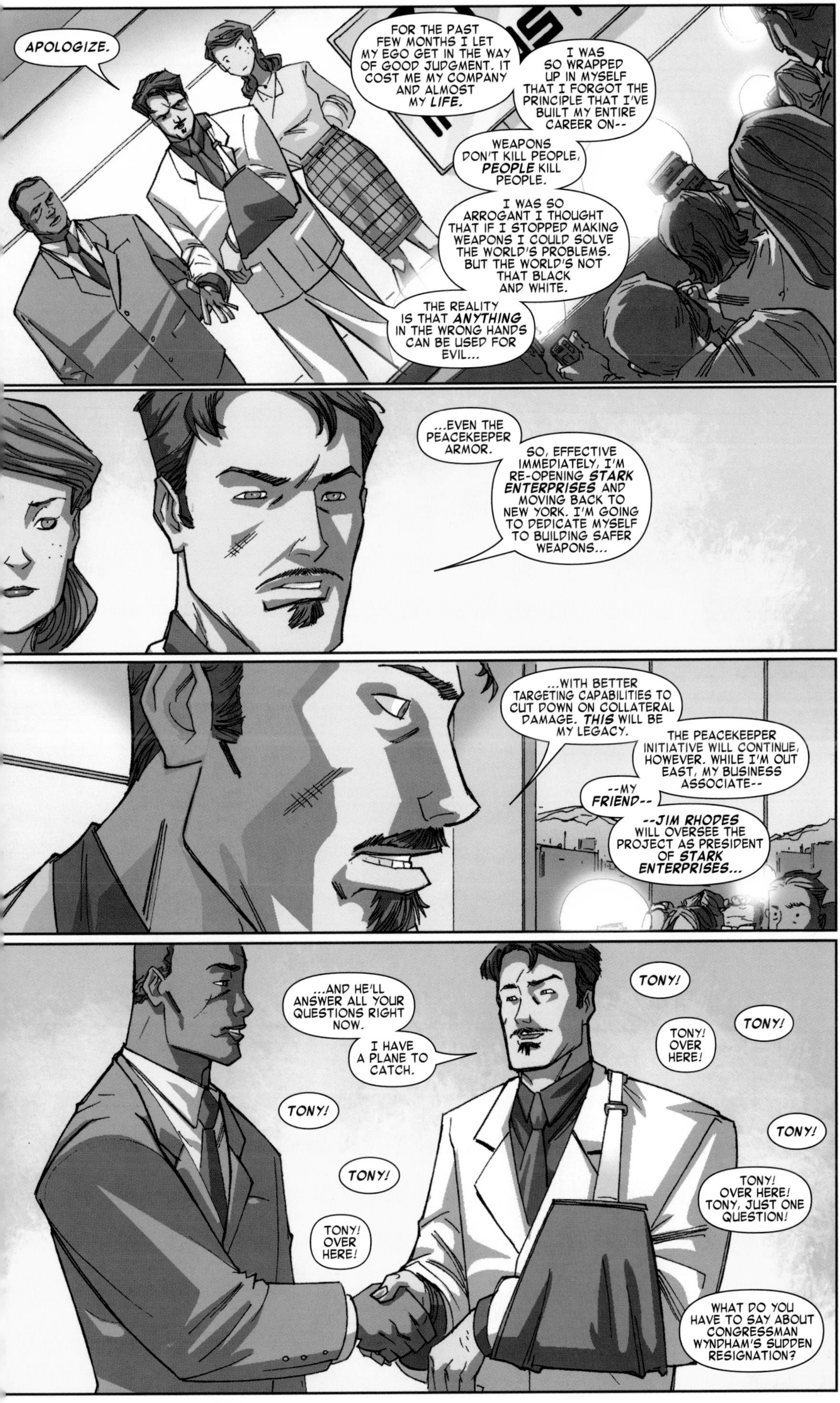
APOLOGIZE.
FOR THE PAST FEW MONTHS I LET MY EGO GET IN THE WAY OF GOOD JUDGMENT. IT COST ME MY COMPANY AND ALMOST MY LIFE.
I WAS SO WRAPPED UP IN MYSELF THAT I FORGOT THE PRINCIPLE THAT I'VE BUILT MY ENTIRE CAREER ON--
WEAPONS DON'T KILL PEOPLE, PEOPLE KILL PEOPLE.
I WAS SO ARROGANT I THOUGHT THAT IF I STOPPED MAKING WEAPONS I COULD SOLVE THE WORLD'S PROBLEMS. BUT THE WORLD'S NOT THAT BLACK AND WHITE.
THE REALITY IS THAT ANYTHING IN THE WRONG HANDS CAN BE USED FOR EVIL...
...EVEN THE PEACEKEEPER ARMOR.
SO, EFFECTIVE IMMEDIATELY, I'M RE-OPENING STARK ENTERPRISES AND MOVING BACK TO NEW YORK. I'M GOING TO DEDICATE MYSELF TO BUILDING SAFER WEAPONS...
...WITH BETTER TARGETING CAPABILITIES TO CUT DOWN ON COLLATERAL DAMAGE. THIS WILL BE MY LEGACY.
THE PEACEKEEPER INITIATIVE WILL CONTINUE, HOWEVER. WHILE I'M OUT EAST, MY BUSINESS ASSOCIATE--
--MY FRIEND--
--JIM RHODES WILL OVERSEE THE PROJECT AS PRESIDENT OF STARK ENTERPRISES...
...AND HE'LL ANSWER ALL YOUR QUESTIONS RIGHT NOW.
I HAVE A PLANE TO CATCH.
TONY!
TONY!
TONY! OVER HERE!
TONY!
TONY!
TONY!
TONY! OVER HERE!
TONY! OVER HERE! TONY, JUST ONE QUESTION!
TONY! OVER HERE!
WHAT DO YOU HAVE TO SAY ABOUT CONGRESSMAN WYNDHAM'S SUDDEN RESIGNATION?

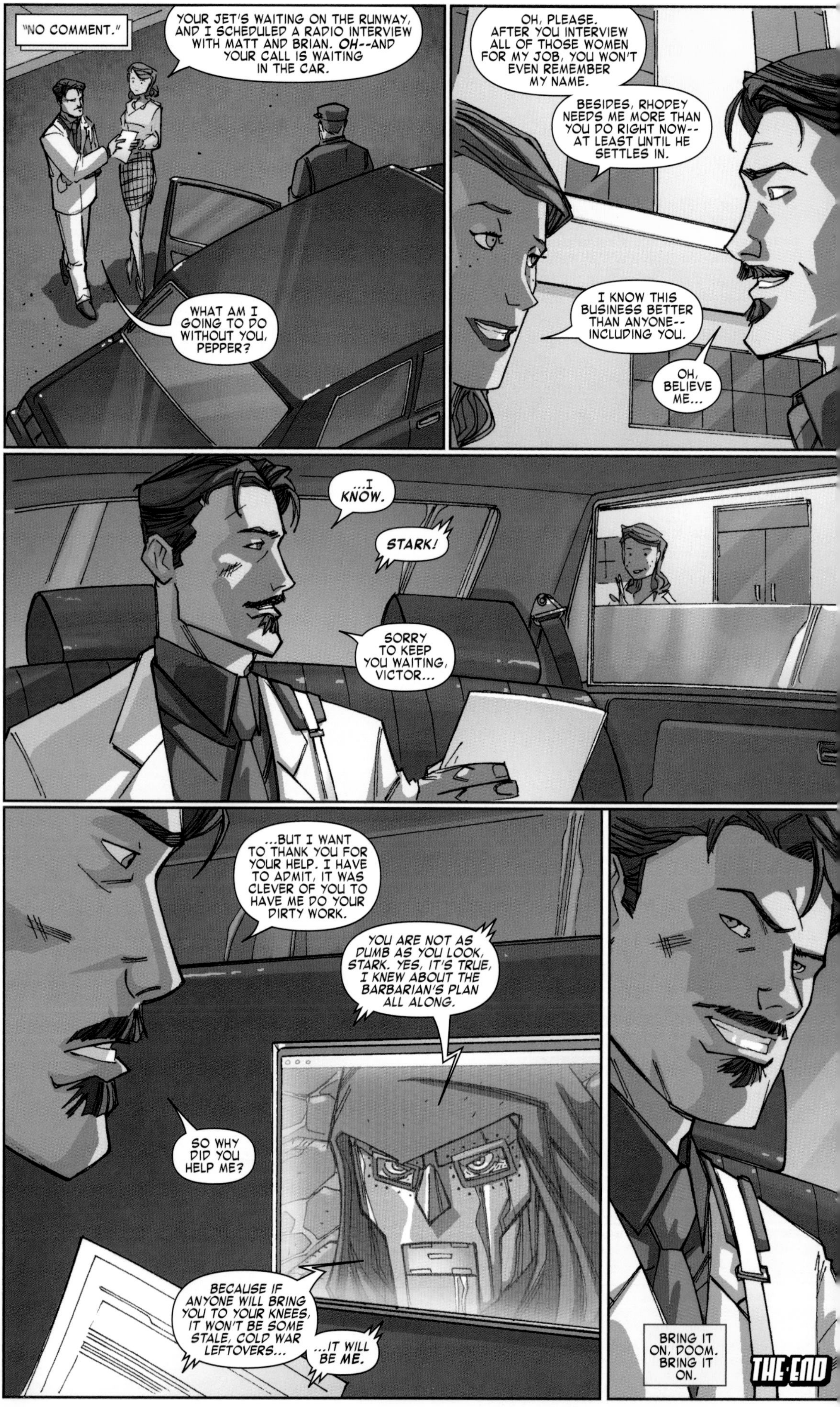
"NO COMMENT."
YOUR JET'S WAITING ON THE RUNWAY, AND I SCHEDULED A RADIO INTERVIEW WITH MATT AND BRIAN. OH--AND YOUR CALL IS WAITING IN THE CAR.
WHAT AM I GOING TO DO WITHOUT YOU, PEPPER?
OH, PLEASE. AFTER YOU INTERVIEW ALL OF THOSE WOMEN FOR MY JOB, YOU WON'T EVEN REMEMBER MY NAME.
BESIDES, RHODEY NEEDS ME MORE THAN YOU DO RIGHT NOW--AT LEAST UNTIL HE SETTLES IN.
I KNOW THIS BUSINESS BETTER THAN ANYONE--INCLUDING YOU.
OH, BELIEVE ME...
...I KNOW.
STARK!
SORRY TO KEEP YOU WAITING, VICTOR...
...BUT I WANT TO THANK YOU FOR YOUR HELP. I HAVE TO ADMIT, IT WAS CLEVER OF YOU TO HAVE ME DO YOUR DIRTY WORK.
YOU ARE NOT AS DUMB AS YOU LOOK, STARK. YES, IT'S TRUE, I KNEW ABOUT THE BARBARIAN'S PLAN ALL ALONG.
SO WHY DID YOU HELP ME?
BECAUSE IF ANYONE WILL BRING YOU TO YOUR KNEES, IT WON'T BE SOME STALE, COLD WAR LEFTOVERS...
...IT WILL BE ME.
BRING IT ON, DOOM. BRING IT ON.
THE END